Select`ed readers from different walks of life and religious backgrounds (Buddhist,` Christian, Hindu, Jain, Jewish, Muslim, Shinto, Sikh, and Zoroastrian) are saying this about the book:

(continued from back cover)

"The precept for a peaceable and harmonious community of Mankind as passionately adumbrated by the author impresses both for its visionary freshness and pragmatic holism. He convincingly shows that demurral with this design for life can only accentuate division and precipitate disaster.

This is not a book one can put down without being imbued with it."
— **PROFESSOR EMERITUS INDU KANT SHUKLA**

"A book that encourages one to sit up and think past the confines of one's narrow, enslaved outlook on what passes for 'religion,' past the hindrances set up by so-called religious leaders in their bigoted complacence is worth testing out in the search for the eternal and the Sufi's musings are a commendable step in that direction."
— **PERVEEZ VICCAJI, WRITER, JOURNALIST**

"When I first saw that this was a religious treatise, I kind of groaned inwardly. Of course I cannot like all kinds of literature equally, but as a critic, I try to be fair and open-minded even if a book is not my favorite genre. But I must say this book held my interest throughout.

It is interesting to contemplate the Sufi's conclusions about God, government, and economics."
— **DIANE G. STELLEY, BOOK CRITIC**

"Time has come to replace the ethnic gods with the One God that encompasses the great wisdom of all religions. This book makes an important contribution toward that end by presenting complex concepts with deeper meaning in simple and easy to understand language."
— **PRAVIN L. KAPADIA, MD, PHYSICIAN**

"The Sufi's ideas keep coming back to me, intruding upon my mind and challenging my long held beliefs.

I have to admit that this little book did change my outlook and gave me a sense of empowerment. I hope it will be translated in other languages."
— **YURIKO MIYAGAWA, BUSINESS OWNER**

"Ideas expressed in this readable, interesting and thought provoking book are at once iconoclastic and affirmative, unifying and liberating. Sufi has blown the conch-shell for the Absolute Oneness of God and the Absolute Universality of Religion."
— **GURJIT SINGH DHALIWAL, MD, PSYCHIATRIST**

"The Sufi has beautifully related [and explained] the concepts of Love, Peace, and Freedom. I fully agree with his idea of the liberation of God from religious bondage.
It is a must read for people of all religions."
— **S. FARRUKH SIYAR, BUSINESS MANAGER**

"What I like most about the book is that it is very thought provoking. It raises issues which need to be discussed [in our society] and presents them in a creative manner."
— **JOHN M. GUSTAFSON, JD, ATTORNEY**

"This book is an eye opener for those [of us] who look at people of other religions and sects with a strange eye. It is a must read for all people of all religions."
— **S. SHAHAB-UL-HAQ, BUSINESS OWNER**

A Sufi's Ruminations On
One World Under God

A Sufi's Ruminations On

One World Under God

John Ishvaradas Abdallah

Star Publications

San Pedro, California, USA

A Sufi's Ruminations on
One World Under God

Copyright © 2002 John Ishvaradas Abdallah

All Rights Reserved. No part of this book may be reproduced or transmitted in any form or by any means, electronic or mechanical, including photocopying, recording or by any information storage and retrieval system without written permission from the author, except for the inclusion of brief quotations in a review.

PUBLISHED BY:

Star Publications

www.star-publications.com
P. O. Box 6175
San Pedro, CA 90734-6175, USA
310-514-2146

Library of Congress Control Number: 2001098580

ISBN 1-885498-48-9: $10.00 Softcover

Printed and bound
in the United States of America

Dedicated to
the spirit of

NICHOLAS
COPERNICUS

who dared to challenge
the conventional wisdom
of his time and space

DISCLAIMER

All characters in this book are fictitious,
and any resemblance to actual persons,
living or dead, is purely coincidental.

SUGGESTION

Please become familiar with the Glossary
before reading the book.

REQUEST FOR RESPONSE

Your comments on the ideas
presented in this book
and any questions you wish included
in the next book will be greatly appreciated.
Please write to the author,
care of the publisher.
Thank you.

CONTENTS

PROLOGUE:	*The Exordium*	*13*
CHAPTER ONE:	An Invitation	*15*
CHAPTER TWO:	The Conversation	*21*
CHAPTER THREE:	Spiritual Awakening	*51*
CHAPTER FOUR:	Surrender As Solution	*89*
EPILOGUE:	*Sermon on the Mount*	*97*

APPENDICES:

1.	The Eightfold Path Through Gautama	*98*
2.	The Ten Commandments Through Moses	*99*
3.	*Surrender* Through Krishna	*100*

GLOSSARY:	*101*
ORDER FORM:	*111*

The Exordium

In The Name of God
The Compassionate
The Merciful

Praise be to God, Lord of the Universe.
The Compassionate, the Merciful,
Sovereign of the Day of Judgment!
You alone we worship,
and to You alone we turn for help.
Guide us to the straight path,
The path of those whom You have favored,
Not of those who incur Your wrath,
Nor of those who go astray.

From *The Koran,* Translated by N. J. Dawood
1990 Penguin Books

CHAPTER ONE

An Invitation

*D*avid Goldstein, my college roommate from some years ago sent me an announcement of a lecture that a mystic would give in Santa Cruz. On the page, David had written a note: "You're always asking questions. Maybe this man has answers. Or maybe not. But do come up if you can and spend a few days with Barbara and me. . . ."

David was surely remembering that in many discussions across the years I raised certain questions about God and religion, but as I looked at the announcement, I did not think that I would find answers from a Sufi. I had not found satisfactory answers from the Christian church in which I was raised or from the teachings of other religions—Eastern or Western—to which I had given considerable study. So, although the thought of visiting David and his wife was appealing, the thought of driving from Los Angeles to Santa Cruz—at a very busy time for me—to hear a Sufi speak made it easy to decline the invitation.

The day after the lecture, I received a call from David, who went directly to his point with the question, "Can you be free on Thursday?"

"Yes," I answered. "I always have the option of working on Saturday."

"Good," he said. "I'm going to give you the opportunity to make up for your error in missing last night's program and to do me a favor at the same time."

With some amusement, I thanked David for his generosity, which he ignored and went on to say that the experience was so special for him that he knew I would find it more so—even with what he called my "cautious and detached attitude about all Western and Eastern thought and religions." David noted that I should find the idea of religion without religion provocative enough but that the speaker's observations about the real world would provide a fresh perspective. "His ideas are so out of the ordinary," David said, "that a student newspaper editorial on an Ivy League campus on the East Coast named him the Fool on the Hill."

Then he explained a complicated schedule that he and the speaker had developed for the next few days. My part would be simply to be host to the speaker for most of one day and to drive him to the Los Angeles Airport in the evening. That was certainly an easy "favor" to do for David, and, if David responded as positively as his words and voice indicated, I thought that I should take the "opportunity."

Thinking ahead to topics and questions for the Sufi, I searched my desk for the announcement David had sent me. It was still there, informing me, among other matters, that Dr. Ashwin Nehru (no relation to the late Prime Minister) was born in India but came to the United States as a graduate student in microbiology. He earned his Masters and Doctorate and became a university professor, teaching and doing research . . .

His wife, Amrita, a poet who was known and respected in literary circles and whose poetry had been published in several magazines, was killed in one of those random and senseless automobile accidents.

Dr. Nehru took a sabbatical and began wandering and meditating. He underwent experiences that changed his personality, his knowledge and understanding, and the way that he lived his life.

He changed his name to Ahimsa, which means "absence of violence," knowing it is a feminine word, to defy gender compartmentalization, and, as Sufi Ahimsa Guruji, has been upsetting and challenging people ever since.

The notes were interesting, if not detailed. I wondered how a Sufi could be a Guru, or vice versa, but I liked the last line; maybe he could speak to me. There was a thin link between us. If he was a "Nehru," he was a Brahmin and Hindu by birth, but there was no indication of religious teaching. My parents were born in India but had little exposure to Hinduism, both being at least third generation Christians. They did learn about languages, customs, and religions of India before they came to the United States to practice medicine, and they passed on to me some knowledge of those matters.

On Thursday morning, when my door bell rang, I opened the door and greeted David, who returned the greeting and said, "Sufiji, I would like to present John Satya Vidyarthi." Ahimsa looked like neither a Guru nor a Sufi—or at least not like the images I held. He was about my height, 5'8", but a little slimmer, no more than 140 pounds. He was wearing well-tailored light gray woolen slacks and a dark jacket.

We chatted for a while. David explained again his reasons for not staying longer and took his leave. I offered some alternative plans, but the Sufi was entirely in accord with my suggestion that we go to an isolated and often empty beach, one not favored by swimmers, surfers, or anglers. I picked folding chairs, blankets, refreshments—everything we could need—and after donning appropriate clothing, we were on our way.

The Sufi graciously consented to my taping our conversation, most of which I now offer you. I had thought very much about what I wanted to ask, and I did raise some of my planned questions, but his answers took me in other directions, also. I have edited the conversation only to ensure a standard of written usage and to eliminate some repetitions and extraneous comments. Rather than try to make a narrative of the dialogue, I have simply indicated which of us is speaking and added a few comments (in italics) about the day.

I ask that you, as reader, indulge my effort and accept the dialogue as an informal and impromptu discussion. I offer it to you because it opened new directions for me. My thinking is now moving out of the circle in which it was caught. If what is written here causes you to think about or to question ideas, concepts, and beliefs, I will be pleased even as the Sufi said that he was pleased to have me as a listener.

If what is written here is instrumental in your achieving a state of being that makes you richer in spirit or in your undertaking actions that make the world a better place, I could ask for no more. I wish you peace and understanding.

CHAPTER TWO

The Conversation

*A*t the beach, we set down all that I had brought with me, spread a blanket, and opened the beach chairs but decided to walk for a while. As we walked, the Sufi told me more about himself, especially about his year of withdrawal, during which he left behind the fascinating world that could be seen only with his microscope and moved to the compelling world that could be seen only with newly cleansed and dedicated senses. He went to cities, where he spent hours reading, studying, observing people. He went to the mountains, where he spent hours thinking, meditating, observing nature, often *seeing no other person for a week. He took a small tent and water—no food—into a remote desert, where, for an unmarked number of days, he looked upward and outward. More often, however, he went to the ocean; there, more than in other places, he could lose himself and find himself.*

When we returned to our spot, I reached for my tape recorder, thanking him once more for allowing me to record our discussion. Again, he was gracious and added that he was pleased when someone listened. Turning on the machine, I took a deep breath and spoke.

John: Sufiji, I have framed many questions for this moment, but now I find that I don't know where to begin.

Sufi: Perhaps I should preface our discussion by saying that I welcome all your questions, but I do not know all the answers. My knowledge is limited. No being other than God has complete knowledge. What I have to offer is the sum of what my special and particular experience revealed to me and of the knowledge and thought that I have applied to my spiritual experience.

John: Then, at what point do you start offering that sum? What is now your belief?

Sufi: My basic and fundamental belief is: "*La ilaha illal Llah; Muhammad Rasool Allah.*" That is,

"There is no god but God; Muhammad is the Messenger of God."

John: So you are a Muslim?

Sufi: Yes. And because I am a Muslim, I am a Zoroastrian, a Hindu, a Buddhist, a Christian, a Taoist, a Jew, a Jain, a Sikh, and so forth.

John: How is that possible?

Sufi: It is. Let me explain. Certainly, there are apparent differences in the doctrines, the rituals, and the customs and cultures of these religions that seem to contradict and oppose one another. But in spite of those differences, we see a common code of conduct. We are instructed to:

- speak truth
- be honest
- do justice
- be compassionate
- be loving
- promote peace
- do good work, and so on.

God, through his last Messenger, Muhammad, says in the Koran that Messengers of God were sent to all people in different lands with different languages, customs, traditions, and levels of understanding at different times throughout human history.

The Koran doesn't name them all, but most

Biblical prophets, such as Abraham, Moses, Jesus, and many others are specifically mentioned as Messengers of God and their stories related. The Books of the Bible—the Old and the New Testaments—are recognized as the Books of God, but they are said to have been changed or altered in ways that incorrectly name Jesus as the Son of God and the Jews as the chosen people.

The Messengers of God and the books that are specifically mentioned in the Koran are all Middle Eastern in origin. But if you read the Vedas, the Upanishads, the Dhammapada, the Tao Te Ching, and other scriptures of the lands beyond the Middle East, you see that it is not just possible but highly probable that Valmiki, Narada, Rama, Krishna, Gautama, Vardhamana, Asoka, Lao-Tse, and many others like them were all Messengers of God. Perhaps only the Koran uses the term "Messenger of God," but all those figures delivered essentially the same message that there is no god but God who alone is worthy of our devotion, worship, and surrender.

John: Sufiji, while I cannot speak for people of other religions, I know Christians will not accept your premise that you can be a Christian without accepting Jesus as the Son of God, or God Himself, and a Savior.

Sufi: I am not suggesting that you accept my premise. I am simply stating my beliefs.

But would you agree that Christianity is a

monotheistic religion and "there is no god but God" another way of stating the first of the Ten Commandments?

John: Of course, Christianity is a monotheistic religion. And I have to admit I didn't realize that the Islamic Creed is simply a variation of the First Commandment. But don't you think the theological concept of the Trinity of God is essential to Christian doctrine?

Sufi: Theology, in my opinion, is an apology for lack of *experience* of the existence of God; it's a useless substitute. Neither any sophisticated doctrine nor any elaborate theology can ever describe, define, or explain sufficiently and completely either God or the existence of God.

John: What about Hinduism? I know that the words "Absolute One," "Supreme Being," "Supreme Self," "Eternal One," and "Only One" throughout the Vedas and the Upanishads seem to support your argument of monotheism, but how can you explain the many gods?

Sufi: I think polytheism made its way in Hinduism for two reasons: First, a zealous group of artists and artisans might have either determined on their own or were hired by others to illustrate and depict through drawings, paintings, and sculptures the words and verses of the Messengers of

God, which were already distorted by the Brahmins of the time. Second, there might have been a conspiracy of the Brahmins and the ruling class of the time to consolidate their own power and privileges, and deny human beings direct access to God and to require intercessors and intermediaries.

Interestingly, the Second of the Ten Commandments, conveyed to us through Moses, specifically forbids graven images. A similar prohibition given to the Rishis may have been deliberately disregarded and concealed by the Brahmins. Nevertheless, in this process, the Brahmins also devised a caste system that persists among the so-called educated because it serves whatever special or particular advantage it offers them over others. I believe such a system of caste could not have been possible without an elaborately conceived system of many gods and polytheism.

It is also possible that the stories using the imagery of gods and goddesses were part of the culture and the language with its phraseology, idioms, and symbolism that prevailed more than 2,500 years ago. If we transpose the gods of Hinduism to a different place and time, vis-à-vis the Abrahamic religions, they become attributes of God, Messengers of God, or angels of God. The trinity of God (Ishvara) in Hinduism, consisting of Brahma, the Creator; Vishnu, the Sustainer; and Siva, the Destroyer, for example, would become simply three, among many, attributes of God. Rama, Krishna, Valmiki, Narada, Vyasa, and many other Rishis would be Messengers of God, making Hinduism one of the oldest monotheistic religions.

Maybe I am going overboard with my imagination, but I wonder whether there is not a spiritual connection between the postures of the Muslim worship *Salat* or *Namaz* and those of *Yoga*. Another mystical and spiritual connection may be between the eternal sound *Aum* and the three Arabic letters *Alif, Laam, Meem* that appear at the beginning of many Surahs or Chapters of the Koran. If we take the predominant sound of each of these Arabic letters and pronounce them together, don't they sound *Aum*?

Whether or not the connection exists, there can be no denying that at the highest spiritual levels, all religions have a connection through time and space.

John: But you are not suggesting that all religions are Islam in reality?

Sufi: I look at Islam as a movement through all religions.

John: What do you mean?

Sufi: "Islam" is an Arabic word for submission or surrender (to God), which is the essence of all religions.

John: The essence of all religions?

Sufi: Yes. The purpose of religion is to provide Man with a comprehensive belief system that will encompass every aspect of life. At the core of this belief system is a spiritual aspect, a need to experience the existence of God, to reach God, to see God, to have communion with God, to be one with God, and so forth. The condition necessary to achieve this state is total absorption, complete surrender. And that's what Islam means.

But the essence of Islam is in the Creed: "*La ilaha illal Llah; Muhammad Rasool Allah.*" The Koran, the Bibles, the Vedas, the Dhammapada, the Upanishads, and all other scriptures and books of God are an elaborate explanation of this declaration of faith.

John: But how?

Sufi: Consider the implied meaning of surrender to the One God in the declaration: "There is no god but God; Muhammad is the Messenger of God." The concept of surrender to no god but (The One) God is the most potent of all the evolutionary and revolutionary ideas that have ever been presented to Man.

As a statement of surrender or submission to that Supreme Power—God—it is the ultimate declaration of independence of Man from every conceivable bondage or servitude that humans impose on themselves and on others. It is a declaration of equality of Man, regardless of gender, color, language, nationality, or occupation.

When Man believes and makes this very simple statement, God offers Man the absolute and total freedom (of will and action) that it is possible for Man to take. It is an invitation to the straight path. I can be free. All I need to do is accept and profess the creed, and I *am* free. I need not submit to anyone, any idea, any force—no matter how big or powerful—on this planet or in this Universe because I have decided to submit to the One, the Only, the Ultimate Power worthy of our submission: God. There are no intercessors, no intermediaries, no smaller gods that I need to submit to. My God is the same One God that each of the Messengers of God submitted to. God has awarded me, very generously, direct access without *any* intermediaries or intercessors.

In fact, only direct access is acceptable; intercessors or intermediaries are not acceptable. They are forbidden. Yes, even Muhammad cannot be an intercessor; he is simply a Messenger. I thank God for choosing Muhammad as a Messenger, and I thank God for choosing Adam, Abraham, Valmiki, Vardhamana, Narada, Gautama, Rama, Krishna, Moses, Jesus, and many others as Messengers before Muhammad.

John: Please, give me a moment to think. We accept the creed of the One God, by which we give ourselves over—or surrender—to the One God, which action then frees us from human constraints and restraints, including the restraint—imposed by self or

by others—that would require us to go through someone else to reach God. Is that too simple a statement
of what you have just said?

Sufi: Not if it helps you to understand the creed.
Indeed, unless and until we *realize* the meaning of
the Creed, we are subject to the whims and wishes
of lesser gods. We are not talking about physical
idols—though they are included. We are talking
about any lesser power that consciously or unconsciously controls our thoughts and actions in some
way. We're talking about parent, child, spouse,
leader, teacher, priest, neighbor, religion, mosque,
temple, church, local government, federal government, computer, car, television set, poverty, wealth,
prestige, fame, pride . . . In fact, anyone, anything,
or any idea that has an influence on thought or
action may be, and usually is, an idol—a lesser
god—visible or invisible until and unless we consciously recognize it and purge it from us.

The *realization* of the meaning of the creed is a
spiritual experience, a "vision of God," so to speak. It
is the most powerful, yet the most humbling experience one can imagine.

The power that is locked up in the creed comes
from the Ultimate Freedom, an attribute of God. But
Freedom is one of the indivisible trinity of attributes
of God; the other two are Love and Peace. One attribute cannot exist without the other two; one is defined
by the other two.

Consider the way these three attributes are inter-woven. Ultimate Freedom belongs to God; God is all Freedom. The freedom that Man is awarded, unlimited in scope from a human perspective as it may be, is still minuscule compared to the Freedom that is God. The freedom that is awarded Man is individual freedom.

As an individual, I have the freedom to think and act as I please. But freedom always comes with responsibility and that makes me humble. The extent to which I can exercise my freedom depends directly and proportionately on the (self) responsibility I accept and fulfill. As part of this responsibility, I must make certain that I do not infringe upon the freedom of my neighbor because, my freedom depends on my neighbor's freedom, just as my neighbor's freedom depends on my freedom. That is the definition of interdependence; it can be experienced only between independent persons.

Now, I will respect my neighbor's freedom only if I am genuinely concerned about and interested in my neighbor's well-being. By definition, genuine concern for and interest in a neighbor's well-being is love. But love of neighbor cannot be experienced unless I have experienced self love; that's what "love thy neighbor as thyself" means.

Ultimate Love belongs to God; God is all Love. The love that Man is awarded, unlimited in scope from a human perspective as it may be, is still minus-cule compared to the Love that is God. The love that is awarded Man is individual (self) love which leads to love of neighbor.

Exercise of individual (self) love and individual freedom (self responsibility) leads to inner peace; love of neighbor and concern for the freedom of the neighbor leads to universal love, universal peace, and collective freedom.

As you can see Love, Peace, and Freedom are so intertwined that they are inseparable. From this trinity of attributes emanate other attributes: Forgiveness, Compassion, Mercy, Justice, and others.

John: Sufiji, I am perplexed. Using your premise, may I say that in the Trinity of Christianity, the Son is Love, the Father is Peace, and the Holy Spirit is Freedom?

Sufi: Certainly. And we can see another metaphor in the Trinity of Ishvara: Brahma as Love, Vishnu as Peace, and Siva as Freedom.

John: I shall require time to digest all that you have just said, but I must say that you are making the *spirit* of religion more meaningful for me.

Sufi: All that I have just said required hours, days, and months for me to postulate. Wait until you have spent more time and thought; then examine everything anew.

John: That I shall. Now, however, maybe it is my turn to go overboard, but it seems to me that you have, in a way, secularized God—that is liberated God from being confined to any one religion.

Sufi: God has always been secular—beyond religions. The God of Abraham, Krishna, Moses, Rama, Lao Tse, Gautama, Jesus, and Muhammad is also the God of Kabir, Nanak, and Gandhi and is the Lord of the Universes and therefore of all people of all religions. It is we who have created barriers among ourselves and between God and us.

John: Barriers?

Sufi: The barriers are gods: gods of race, nationality, gender, color, language, occupation, caste, religion itself, and so on. Each barrier that divides people is also a barrier between us and God.

John: So worship of the One God of Love, Peace, and Freedom removes those barriers?

Sufi: Yes, but it is the exclusivity of the worship that is of utmost importance. Any corruption or compromise of this exclusivity, however insignificant in one's opinion or estimation, is tantamount to idol worship—polytheism.

John: And by idol worship you mean?

Sufi: Idol worship can take many forms, sometimes visible, often not so visible. Essentially, it is worship of the created – created by God or Man. Mostly, it is worship of our own creation and this is not so visible. It is a feeling of superiority at the expense of others; a destructive pride in our own prowess; adoration of ourselves and demand of others to accept us and our creation as supreme; a demand of others to surrender to us. Then there is the visible idolatry of any of God's creation, such as the worship of the Sun, a tree, or a Man.

John: But Sufiji, why so dogmatic? So strict? Why is there no room for some compromise? What is wrong with the concept of God incarnate? That God came and lived among us as a human being like Krishna, Rama, or Jesus?

Sufi: The question is why must God ever be incarnate? Whatever answer you give presupposes a need or a desire by God to have lived and died among us as a human being to accomplish something. I think it is contradictory with an Omnipresent, Omnipotent, Eternal God—the Giver and the Taker of Life, the Creator, the Sustainer, and the Destroyer of Worlds— to have such a desire or need to accomplish something. I think it makes God too small.

It also belittles God to say that God made Man in the image of God. I think it elevates Man's status beyond reason and is an act of self worship, that is idol worship, which prevents Man from even attempting to know God.

From another perspective, it is simply a cop-out. Pardon the expression, but nothing describes the phenomenon better. The lives of the Messengers of God are lives to emulate; the path they have shown is the path to follow. But by calling them God-incarnate, Man begins to devise a scheme to be able to say: "I cannot emulate God. I can't walk in God's footsteps because I am not God."

"There is no god but God" is a principle and a formula for a life of freedom. It ceases to be a principle if compromised; compromise of the principle is compromise of freedom.

Compromise also opens the way for corruption, and any corruption leads to more corruption. To prevent corruption and to preclude loss of the principle and of freedom, we must surrender totally—give complete devotion—to the one God.

Recall Krishna, conveying the message of God: "Give Me your mind and give Me your heart, give Me your offerings and your adoration; and thus with your soul in harmony, and making Me your goal supreme, you shalt in truth come to Me."

And recall Satan offering all the kingdoms of the world and their glory to Jesus if Jesus would worship him. Jesus wouldn't compromise, saying, there is no god but God, who alone is worthy of worship and service.

John: Sufiji, allow me to be the devil's advocate

for a moment. What is wrong with the kingdoms of the world with all its glory?

Sufi: It is all metaphorical. Inherent in the concept of the worship of Satan is polytheism; Satan offers a panoply of attractive idols in the form of "things" to desire, possess, own, cherish, adore, and think about ceaselessly.

The outcome of polytheism or idol worship is injustice, inequity, rivalry, envy, destructive competition, hate, war, exploitation, et cetera.

John: Please excuse my ignorance, but how does polytheism result in all these evils of injustice and inequity?

Sufi: Let's begin with life. We come into and leave this world without our will; we have absolutely no control over our own birth or death. We may believe we have some control over the timing of our own death, but that may only be an illusion. ·

It is between these two events that we gradually acquire our own free will either to worship the Power (God) that brings us into as well as removes us from this world or to worship lesser powers (gods) created and empowered by us. The result of surrendering our freedom to these lesser powers is loss of self-respect and self-esteem. That in turn results in the creation of false self-esteem and self-respect by putting down others and seeking advantage over fellow human beings through exploitation, discrimination, domination, et cetera. Accumulating wealth, power, and prestige is another device to compensate for the loss of self-respect. Thus, it is the cause of many an evil such as injustice, inequity, intolerance, et cetera.

True self-respect comes only from surrendering yourself to the God who has power over life and death. Because it is in the surrender to the Lord of the Worlds that Man can experience maximum freedom. Self-respect and self-esteem come from freedom thus awarded us by God; no amount of wealth, power, and prestige can compensate for the loss of self-esteem and self-respect.

John: Then why does Man seek false self-respect?

Sufi: Perhaps because false respect is more glamorous for Man; it is the glory of the world.

John: Why?

Sufi: I believe it is intertwined with the purpose and the meaning of life. Often, purpose and meaning are defined in terms of acquisition and accumulation of wealth and material goods. The underlying assumption is that there is nothing beyond this life, beyond the material existence. In our own time, acquisition and accumulation of wealth have, more than ever, become highly desirable goals and the very purpose of life. Quality of life is measured in material comfort that wealth can buy; the key word, we are told, is "choices." The result is, literally, a vicious cycle of surrendering to more and more smaller gods and seeking to regain the continuing loss of self esteem and self respect. Having "choices" of innumerable gods has become the new meaning of life.

John: Some people believe there is neither purpose in nor meaning of life. But I remember hearing, in my childhood, that the purpose of life is to serve God. In Buddhism, I believe, it is Nirvana, literally, extinction, but figuratively to be One with God. But how do you serve God? Be one with God? Those terms are vague and subject to different interpretations. What do you think is the purpose of life?

Sufi: Man has been searching for the answers since time immemorial. To a large extent, all of Man's religions are a response to that question. What differentiates us as human beings from other forms of life is the search itself; in fact, it is the journey for the search that makes us human. Any answer you get from anyone should only spur you on to search and discover for yourself. It is my observation that most people choose not to search. Of the few that do, most give up too soon too easily. Those who persist are rewarded with the discovery that there is more to life than material existence, that there is continuity of life beyond this phase on Earth. The search itself never ends because the search for the purpose and meaning of life is a search for God. How can the search for the Infinite One and the Eternal One ever end?

I believe the purpose of life is to experience the existence of God, that is Love, Peace, and Freedom. The meaning of life is realized in sharing that experience with others. Both of those statements are derived from the same fundamental principle of life: "There is no god but God."

John: A popular American word for anything which is entirely positive, appealing, and satisfying is "beautiful," and I would say that your statement of what you believe is, indeed, beautiful. But is there no room for a different belief?

Sufi: Of course, there is room for other beliefs. I am telling you today what my experience and my study—including a year of intense experience and study—led me to believe. I express my beliefs because I am committed to them.

Let me make two points about religious belief. First, we must speak of the relationship between Man and God. That is the purely spiritual aspect which allows Man to seek enlightenment, to experience the existence of God. Certainly, your experience may be different from my experience. We may, therefore, have different perceptions of God; we may disagree about perceptions of God. You, as a Christian in the traditional sense of the word, have the right and freedom to believe that Jesus is the Son in an otherwise indivisible Trinity of God. Or, if you were a Hindu and preferred to worship as god what I believe to be an attribute of God, or if you were a follower of any religion and preferred to interpret literally what I consider to be a metaphor, you should have the freedom to do so as I do. If a method, path, or conception of your choice helps you experience the existence of God, so much the better.

Second, we must speak of the relationship between Man and Man. As long as your belief does not infringe on my freedom, I have nothing to fear. If you do not love your neighbor (regardless of your neighbor's belief) as you love yourself and you infringe upon your neighbor's freedom (and peace), then there is a problem that needs discussion and resolution. A democratic government (one of laws) provides a resolution which assures the safeguarding of everyone's freedom and equity. Thus, government replaces the old religions—and for good reason.

Conversely, we should be able to say that if a belief does not prompt and promote love, peace, and freedom, there may be something wrong with the first aspect: the perception of God.

John: Those are important and useful statements, and I do want to consider some examples, but, lest I forget, I want to go back to what you were saying about polytheism. Does it follow that we, who call ourselves Christians, have indeed given in to the Satan?

Sufi: It certainly appears that way; as if we have

established the very kingdom that Satan so outra-
geously tempted Jesus with. My home, USA, seems to
have become a haven of idol worshipers. But it is not
just the Christians. We all seem to be caught in a kind
of polytheism that requires us to deny it even while we
practice it and profess another faith.

John: So we are hypocrites.

Sufi: Yes. Perhaps unconsciously or unknowingly
but hypocrites nevertheless. And we can begin to undo
the damage by simply resolving to follow the First
Commandment, 'Thou shall have no other gods
before Me.'

John: What would happen if we were to surrender to the One God—the only God—and to discover
the purpose and the meaning of life: to *experience* the
existence of God and share with others love, peace,
and freedom?

Sufi: We would be establishing the Kingdom of
God on Earth, which is the same as an Islamic State or
a Rama Rajya.

John: What would it look like?

Sufi: In the Kingdom of God on Earth, Mankind is
but one community. There are no distinctions or privileges based on color of skin, gender, language,
nationality, or any other such aspect. Neither laws nor
boundaries are needed in this Islamic State because

everyone is respectful of the rights of others. This Rama Rajya under One God is certainly a secular democracy in which matters of importance, matters for individual and common good, are decided by consensus. It is a world of nonviolence, a world in which weapons of destruction have been destroyed because no one needs them anymore. It is a world of economic equity in which no one wants to be wealthy, and accumulation of wealth is considered a lowly desire and worship of a small god. It is a world in which everyone is satisfied with material necessities sufficient to pursue a spiritual life in search of God—Love, Peace, and Freedom.

John: But Sufiji, isn't that some kind of Utopia?

Sufi: True. And fortunately neither of us is so naive as to believe it is at hand, or some might say, even possible. However, that should not discourage us from preparing for one, that is, working toward establishing one.

John: That is a worthy and a noble goal, but does it make sense to pursue an impossible dream?

Sufi: It makes a lot more sense than whatever else we are doing right now. Of course, we live our physical lives in terms of the physical world. But there is often difficulty in trying to determine what action is best. And when two or three actions seem equally practicable, we must make choices. Leaders of nations argue about what will work for nations. Individuals struggle to find what will work in their lives. In the process, nations and individuals find what is practicable—or more likely, what is desirable—and the pursuit of whatever they find comes to dominate and control their lives. Without an ultimate goal to guide them, without the one God to give them direction, they give themselves to lesser gods. Thus, it is pursuing wealth or a higher standard of living or even a longer life that in and of itself makes no sense to me.

John: There is no sense even in pursuing longer life?

Sufi: If so, the sense is quite limited. It is one thing to lead hygienic and healthy lives but quite another to try to prolong life by all means, usually by surrendering to many a god of technology.

John: Sufiji, that seems to me a little extreme.

Sufi: I am sure it does. It seemed extreme to me when it first occurred to me. But think about it. Is the purpose of our life to prolong life?

I wonder if it is the fear of death that drives our desire to postpone it as long as possible. Ironically, in seeking this postponement, we miss the precious opportunity to seek the God who gave us life. We don't seem to realize that there can be no life without death. Maybe it is the love of the material world, that is, love of every *thing* in our lives that makes us blind and oblivious to the spiritual.

John: But you are not suggesting that we stop learning, stop pursuing knowledge, are you?

Sufi: No. Just the opposite. We very much need knowledge. You, as a Christian, are accustomed to reciting, "And you shall know the truth, and the truth shall make you free." We must pursue knowledge. It is the misapplication of knowledge that we need to be concerned about. A short life of love, peace, and freedom in surrender to God is better than a long life in bondage to many a smaller god.

John: Sufiji, in my own case, if it were not for the advances in medical technology, I would have died a long time ago and many times since.

Sufi: John, the same is true with me, but that was before I came to this realization.

Let us focus for a moment on what you just said: "If it were not for the advances in medical technology, I would have died a long time ago and many times since." You are stating a widely accepted notion or belief that "technology" saves lives or that "we" save lives with the help of technology that we created.

Do you realize what that means?

John: Yes. I realize that in terms of what you have been saying we are, in one instance, treating technology as god and in the other ourselves as gods. In either case, we are worshipping ourselves, which is what idol worship is all about.

Sufi: Exactly.

John: Would it make a difference if instead of saying, "if it were not for the technology," we say, "if it were not for God who made it possible for us to have the technology"?

Sufi: Yes, I think it would make a big difference— if the change of words expresses genuine belief. It would then rightly show our dependence on God who alone deserves all credit and praise.

But even if the belief is genuine, we still can't escape the question, "Is prolonging life the purpose of life?"

John: Even if it is not the purpose of life as such, we can argue that it is not in opposition to the purpose and may even be complementary.

Sufi: How may it be complementary?

John: By prolonging life, I will have more time and more opportunities to experience the existence of God.

Sufi: Is that the intent? Are you seeking more time and opportunities to seek God? Are you desiring a spiritual experience? I think the answer to these questions will determine whether technology is a gift of mercy from God or a god itself that has become a barrier between you and God.

John: Is it all right to use medical technology to alleviate the suffering of a child?

Sufi: Certainly. The child is still dependent on the parents or adult guardians, and whatever knowledge God has given us may be used to alleviate the suffering. But even as we are doing it, we should be mindful of the blessings of God and remain focused on the purpose of life.

John: Let's move from medical technology to other technologies. What do you think about the continuing advances and developments in production and preservation of food, in communication, and other scientific knowledge?

Sufi: The same principle applies. If we praise and credit technology for improving our lives, as is often done, we make gods out of technologies and suffer the consequences of idol worship. On the other hand, if we credit, thank, and praise God for teaching us technology *and* remain focused on the purpose of life to seek God, we are most likely to start doing away with unnecessary technology and begin reducing the harmful and undesirable side effects of technological development. It would then be possible, eventually, to eliminate pollution of our environment, our bodies, and our minds and to reverse the effects of carcinogens and other harmful agents that technology so readily—and so ignorantly—unleashes.

John: Therefore our intent or motive is most important.

Sufi: Yes. Gautama, the Messenger of God, summarized it best with his Eightfold Path that begins with Right Knowledge followed by Right Attitude. I think Right Knowledge that "there is no god but God" alone leads us to the Right Attitude.

John: Then is Right Knowledge alone sufficient in and of itself?

Sufi: A person who has *experienced* the existence of God, that is, one who has been exposed to the Right Knowledge, will know the right way to live. The Eightfold Path[1] as revealed to Gautama and the Ten Commandments[2] as revealed to Moses should be more than adequate to enable one to live a life in pursuit of God. A person who learns and practices the right way to live and has a genuine and focused desire to see God is most likely to be rewarded with vision of the Divine. One leads to the other.

John: Sufiji, given the way the world is now around us, I am not very optimistic that Man will heed

---

[1]See Appendix 1

[2]See Appendix 2

any advice about the spiritual. Man is too proud of his scientific achievements, the technological progress, material comforts, and a variety of distracting amusement and entertainment to do anything more than to continue to pay ritualistic lip service to God and the spiritual. Over three thousand years of history are witness to Man's refusal to accept and be content with a moderate material life even though that would—as all religions have taught us—make possible the pursuit of the spiritual.

Sufi: While I agree with your observation, I do not share your pessimism; on the contrary, I am quite optimistic.

~

Sufiji paused as I changed the tape in the recorder, and I offered him some refreshments. From my basket I took a large thermos of tea and some fruits and nuts, which he seemed to enjoy. For a few minutes, we talked about food and nutrition. As might be guessed, Ahimsaji practiced moderation and careful selection in all that he consumed. He was not a vegetarian, but he avoided highly processed food insofar as possible.

The Sufi was more interested in talking about the pull and the power of the ocean than about food, for the ocean provided a spiritual renewal and sustenance more important to him than meeting physical needs. We sat in silence for a while. My mind was occupied

*with all that we had discussed. I realized that what
Sufiji was saying was definitely speaking to me, and I
also realized that what he was saying came from deep
inside. It was more than knowledge gained from dili-
gent study. I could not escape the thought that he was
speaking as one who—as he had said only minutes
before—"has experienced the existence of God," and
had done so in a way that I had not.*

*As reluctant as I was to intrude on his thoughts, I
felt some urgency to continue our dialogue and said as
softly as I could, "You were speaking of your optimism
in the face of Man's destruction of the earth." He
smiled, dropped his head for a moment, and continued.*

CHAPTER THREE

Spiritual Awakening

Sufi: Yes. I believe the world is yearning for spiritual awakening. Perhaps Man is beginning to feel that unharnessed and often irresponsible advancement of the material world has compromised the spiritual in some significant ways. Progress has been neither all good nor all bad, but the balance between the spiritual and the material has tipped too much in favor of the material. Effects are showing up everywhere: in the vast disparity of wealth, increase in drug use, crime, general lawlessness, gangs, corruption, dishonesty on a much larger scale than ever before. Those and other symptoms and ills associated with idol worship arise from a very elaborate, intricate, and sophisticated new religion: Capitalism.

John: Capitalism is a religion?

Sufi: Perhaps not in the traditional sense of the word. More appropriately, a pseudo- or a quasi-religion, but a highly effective one. Think about it. Consult a dictionary; you'll find religion defined in terms such as "a system of beliefs and practices generally agreed upon by a number of persons," or "uniting its adherents in a community." By such definitions, Capitalism is not only the religion of choice but the only religion actually being practiced here in these United States of America. As its name implies, Capital or Wealth is the god. Capitalism surely has its own caste or class system, not too different from the outlawed but still practiced caste system of Hinduism. The Capitalists are members of the Ruling or the Warrior class. There is a priestly class of Theologians and Pundits called Economists. Then there is a missionary class of Marketers and Advertisers whose job it is to awaken and arouse dormant desires (gods) and create new ones that never were.

The key message or creed of this modified religion is "Consume." Waste is its by-product. New movements of the consumer class have sprung up everywhere, trying to introduce ethical standards and values into a religion that seeks cheap labor as obligatory sacrifice, measures the value of human life in dollars and cents, and considers accumulation of wealth and capital as the most desirable virtue.

Using a benign pseudonym, "economic system," it replaced—with little resistance—all our belief systems and religions. Virtually incompatible with all of the world's great religions, it has been presented, deceptively, as neutral and sometimes even complementary to all faiths and religions. Today, the whole world is in awe of its wonder and is embracing it as the newly discovered path to salvation.

John: I know you are talking about a global phenomenon, but if Capitalism is a religion, then it has become a State religion. That creates a problem in the United States because the First Amendment specifically prohibits Congress from making laws concerning establishment of religion. And much of the debate in the United States Congress and in state legislatures is about measures designed to promote and protect Capitalism.

Sufi: That is a very good point, but, unfortunately, people do not see the reality.

John: If a majority of people did see Capitalism as the religion of idol worship, that would call for a court test that could upset the system in very complex ways.

Sufi: The prospect of such a case is amusing to contemplate, but without any idea of what legal rulings might be, I will say that no ruling would end modern polytheism or idol worship.

John: Why not?

Sufi: Because, if my observations are valid, Man by his very nature is polytheistic, idolatrous. It is in the context of *this* "Original Sin" that the acts, not just the concepts, of *repentance* and *redemption*—emphasizing the individual responsibility aspects requiring a change from within—make sense and become important. Why else would we need Messengers— Redeemers, by virtue of informing and warning— with the messages of Monotheism from God? But just as love and Monotheism cannot be legislated in, hate and idol worship cannot be legislated out of existence either.

John: Is Socialism or Communism any better than Capitalism?

Sufi: No. In a way they are all the same. They are three sects of the same religion—Materialism. As Catholicism is to Christianity, so is Capitalism to Materialism; Socialism and Communism are simply the Protestant movements of Capitalism.

John: Communism seems to be on the way out. Even Communist China is experimenting with Capitalism. Do you think we are about to see the end of Communism soon?

Sufi: Yes. Let us hope that the Leninist and Maoist Communism have seen the end of their day. But Marx's Socialism, which is the true Protestant movement of Capitalism, is making inroads into even Capitalist United States. I suspect that most nations will seek some sort of balance between these two powerful religions and may adopt a hybrid called Socialist Capitalism or Capitalist Socialism, depending on which one has a slight edge in its favor at any given time, but the battles and the war between the two will go on.

John: Will go on until one has overcome the other?
Sufi: Until we have seen the end of this epoch—this "Civilization."

John: Do you mean to say that we're seeing the beginning of the end of Western Civilization?
Sufi: Yes. There is absolutely no doubt in my mind. But I don't like to characterize it as *Western* Civilization. I think we have to move beyond East and West and break down all such barriers that divide us into tribes, races, nations, colors, genders, religions, and linguistic groups. We have to start realizing that there is only one history of humankind—spread out over time and space. I am the descendent of the slave and of the king; descendant of the black and of the white; descendant of the Hindu and of the Muslim.

Your history is my history; my history is your history. It is all our history and is good for only one reason: to learn our lesson from it and move on, neither holding others hostage to it nor being held hostage by it.

John: Sufiji, you used the word "lesson," not "lessons." Is there only one lesson to be learned from history?

Sufi: There are more, but there is one most important lesson to be learned: Like Man, like all life, Civilizations also die. This Civilization is not and cannot be an exception. The death of a civilization is not easily perceptible even though signs of decay and the impending end have always been evident, as they are now, but Man is susceptible to denial of his mortality.

John: And present signs are?

Sufi: Signs are invariably the same in each epoch: widespread idol worship and all the inevitable resultant evils.

John: Then all the civilizations of the past ended because of idol worship?

Sufi: Yes. Each and every one of them.

John: But if we have an enlightened Mankind and start a new civilization now—establish the Kingdom of God on Earth— shouldn't that follow the same law of birth and death?

Sufi: The Kingdom of God on Earth, the Rama Rajya, or the Islamic State, as long as it remains one and doesn't fall back on idol worship, will continue as long as the world does. In other words, if it doesn't cease to be the Kingdom of God, it will not die because even for Man, death is simply a gate to pass through to another life—the so-called life after death—so that this world, this life, or this civilization is simply a passing phase, not the end in itself.

I should add that I am using the word "civilization" in deference to common usage and terminology that simply make us feel good. In reality, Mankind has seen only sparks of civilization surrounding the time and space of the Messengers of God. True civilization will begin when the Kingdom of God is established.

John: Sufiji, why haven't any of the monotheistic religions raised any voice against this idol worship and the polytheistic religions?

Sufi: For all practical purposes, the modern polytheistic religion, materialism, has replaced all the great monotheistic religions such as Zoroastrianism, Hinduism, Buddhism, Judaism, Taoism, Christianity, Islam, and others; those good old religions are all dead—as they ought to be. And the dead don't raise any voice.

John: Dead as they ought to be? What do you mean?

Sufi: Religions, like civilizations, die a natural death whether or not they serve the purpose for which they were created. But we don't recognize their death because we don't want to. There may be a sense of guilt that we may be the ones responsible for the demise. Also, it is easier to be in a constant state of denial than to go through a grieving process and move on to build new, timely institutions. So we build monumental tombs in honor of these institutions and worship them as if they were gods. It fits in well and plays into the hands of the modern polytheistic religions.

John: But why do they die?

Sufi: Because they fail to adapt to change. They become fixed and rigid in the time and space of the past. *That* is a sign of death for religions and institutions.

History of religions is really the history of a single movement that is separated by time and space, each religion standing like a marker. The movement is Islam, and the markers are the religions Hinduism, Judaism, Buddhism, Taoism, Christianity, et cetera.

John: So we are divided among ourselves over a dead issue.

Sufi: You couldn't have put it in a better perspective.

John: But why can't we see it? I am beginning to see it now, but why couldn't I see it before?

Sufi: That is the power of illusions.

John: Illusions? What illusions?

Sufi: Consider the most common and obvious illusions: sunrise and sunset. Less than five hundred years ago, Copernicus broke our illusion that the sun and the planets are revolving around the earth. We know now that the earth completes a full rotation on its axis in twenty-four hours, and takes a year to complete a revolution around the sun. But does the naked eye believe it? We still see, and our vocabulary confirms it, sunrise and sunset, meaning the *apparent* rising and the *apparent* descent of the sun, implying the sun revolving around the earth!

Or, consider the sky full of stars at night. The stars "disappear" as the "sun rises;" one illusion creating another. Of course, we know that the stars are still there, but blinded by the sunlight, neither we see them nor are they in our conscious mind. In other words, we have to be consciously aware of the reality in order to see it through the illusion.

So it is with illusions that abound but are not so obvious. For example, we have to constantly and consciously remind ourselves of the truth that we all are one, to see through the *apparent* differences of gender, color, race, tribe, nationality, and religion. We have to make spiritual use and sense of the scientific knowledge to see a globe *despite* its apparent flatness, or to see one planet despite *apparent* lines and boundaries on its surface.

Now, going back to religion, in addition, for a great majority of us, when we talk about "my religion," or "our religion," we mean the religion of our parents, that is, the religion we are "born into." We tend to take our religion as hereditary as black hair or blue eyes.

I think "our religion" becomes more nearly a test of loyalty and duty to our parents than anything else. Like a great family secret, an honor, a tradition, or a crown bestowed upon us through intricate rituals and elaborate ceremonies, we are expected to carry this unique flag of religious identity with pride and exclusivity. Otherwise, we let ourselves, our parents, and through extension, our families, our communities, and sometimes our nations down and bring shame on them all.

So we are given a burden, instead of a responsibility, that we had no idea we were being groomed for and had neither any inclination for nor enough knowledge about. That burden is bound to create anxiety and resentment toward our own folk and community that can be more easily expressed against and transferred to other religions and people of other faiths than our own. That's where the seeds of fanaticism are. Of course, not everyone becomes a fanatic. Many begin and continue a lifelong process of, what I call, justification of one's own faith and denigration of the faith of others.

As one such person, I may or may not study my

own religion, may or may not learn the meaning behind the rituals and the ceremonies but certainly learn all the outward, often superficial signs, symbols, and talk of the religion to justify the authenticity, the exclusivity, the uniqueness, and often the superiority of my own faith. I know little or nothing about other religions. When and if I do, my knowledge is usually based on half-truths or falsehoods. Sometimes my attitude toward them is outright demeaning and insulting.

So we end up closed and narrow-minded, locked in a prison of our own making. All such fault-finding and condemning of each other's religions benefit only the modern polytheism, and we get blindsided by idol worship.

John: Then why don't the learned of each religion—the ministers, the priests, the Brahmins, the rabbis, the caretakers of temples, the mullahs, and others who enjoy a degree of authority and leadership in their own religious communities, encourage people to learn about other religions?

Sufi: The same reasons apply to them, too. After all, they are us; we are them. Mostly, it is ignorance of their own religions as well as ignorance of other religions that prevents them from playing such a role. Their own self-interest may also play a subconscious motive because they would lose the position in their respective communities if they were not promoting the exclusive superiority of their own religion.

John: So they are not very helpful.

Sufi: Much more than not being helpful, they are a major hindrance to enlightenment. Seldom claiming to be intercessors between God and us, they nevertheless act as if they were and, more importantly, are treated as such by a great majority who rely solely on their interpretations. Often, they have turned the Almighty God into a puny god confined within the narrow boundaries of a (dead) religion because of their own narrow mindedness and ignorance. Our challenge is to enlighten them with love, peace, and freedom. Liberated from the shackles of false gods, including religions, they could become a formidable force in the establishment of Kingdom of God on Earth.

John: Then what is our religiosity—our going to churches, synagogues, temples, and mosques—all about?

Sufi: It has simply become one more idol among many. It is also the worship of the dead. Our fear of death seems to transcend life. And the language speaks for itself. Everywhere, there is talk of "revival and revivalism." We all recognize that these good old religions need to be "revived." But we should know, and I think subconsciously we do know, that we cannot revive the dead. The sooner we bring that knowledge to our consciousness and accept it, the better it will be for us all because behind it all, barely visible, is a longing for the spiritual, devoid of old religions.

John: Isn't secularism performing that function?

Sufi: The Godless secularism that is practiced today in the United States and copied elsewhere in the world is, in effect, a distortion of Christianity. Its origin, I believe, lies in the dictum of separation of Church and State, to put into practice an interpretation of what Jesus is reported to have said: give to Caesar (that is emperor or government) what belongs to Caesar and to God what belongs to God.

Moving from there to the American Revolution in the Eighteenth Century, CE, you cannot help but notice the similarity of the theme in the First Amendment: "Congress shall make no law respecting the establishment of religion, or preventing the free exercise thereof."

Ironically, while successfully keeping any one particular old religion out, it let a new one in through the back door and thus institutionalized hypocrisy.

John: But how? What do you mean?

Sufi: As you pointed out yourself earlier, is it not ironical that Congress would establish and make laws to promote and protect Capitalism—the new polytheistic religion? Furthermore, by not acknowledging Capitalism as a religion, even when it has all the trappings of a religion, and claiming that we may practice any religion of our choice, hasn't the Congress institutionalized hypocrisy?

John: It certainly seems that way. But surely you don't think the authors of the Bill of Rights intended it this way?

Sufi: No, I don't think so. But I do think it all began with the distorted interpretation of what Jesus meant.

John: What do you think he meant?

Sufi: In the light of his life and mission, we can interpret or understand it in one of two ways.

First, as the story is related, he looked at the coin and knew it was the picture of the idol and the idol worshipper Caesar, so he said "Give it back to the idol worshipper and come with me because you don't need wealth to find God and the Kingdom of God." In fact, on another occasion, Jesus said it was impossible for a wealthy person to get into God's domain.

Second, Jesus knew, as did every Messenger of God before him, that to God belong the East and the West, the North and the South, the Man and the Beast, and everything that is in the Earth, on the Earth, and in the Universes; there is nothing whatsoever that doesn't belong to God.

John: But Sufiji, surely the separation of Church and State has been good for us. Otherwise, we might have been subjected to a very narrow and outdated interpretation of the Christian religion that would have resulted in an oppressive government.

Sufi: Yes, I agree with you. And we don't need to go very far to see the disastrous results of such religious states in the so-called Islamic countries.

My objection to the Godless secularism is that it is not only Godless, it is full of smaller gods; in other words, the One God has been replaced by a plethora of smaller gods and the resultant idol worship.

In the Islamic countries, we have, in addition, tyranny of despots under the deceitful protection of the so-called Islamic laws. In fact, the situation in these so-called Islamic countries is worse than in countries with Godless secularism resulting in, as you correctly perceived, very oppressive governments covertly practicing and promoting idol worship, all under the shameful guise of Islam.

John: Shameful guise of Islam?

Sufi: Yes. These states have absolutely nothing to do with Islam.

More than a religion, Islam is a movement through time and space for all times and spaces, encompassing the material, the spiritual, the social, the political, and all other aspects of life and the world of Man. The Koran says that this movement started with Adam, the first human and the first Messenger of God. Through the millennia, God sent thousands of Messengers to Man in different parts of the world and at different times, as evidenced by such Messengers as Abraham, Zoroaster, Moses, Narada, Rama, Krishna,

Vardhamana, Gautama, Jesus, and finally Muhammad and through such books of God or scriptures as the Vedas and the Upanishads, the Old and the New Testaments of the Bible, the Dhammapada, and finally the Koran. In a way, the Koran is the affirmation of all of Man's religions and a record of historical progression of the movement that is Islam. More than a book of rigid laws that have not changed over the millennia, the Koran is a book of guidance for further progression of the movement.

Several things happened that would stop and essentially freeze the Islamic movement with the death of the Messenger Muhammad.

The laws that were meant for a specific space and time were interpreted as being for all times and spaces and thus set in stone. The new Muslims themselves accepted the premise proposed by the non-Muslims that a religion was founded by Messenger Muhammad. The deterioration that began during the reign of the Caliph Othman (Osman) corrupted the concept and the system of government with the introduction of nepotism. And then finally the hypocrites Ommayad and his son Yazid extinguished the flame of the movement, a flame which has not burned since that time. That, in a nutshell, is the sad story of the Islamic movement after Messenger Muhammad.

John: Sufiji, are you suggesting that the generally recognized history of Islam is not really the history of Islam?

Sufi: Precisely. Robbers, thugs, thieves, and murderers who called themselves Rulers, Monarchs, Kings, and Lords took the name of Islam for their own self interests. In the guise of promoting, safeguarding, or establishing Islam, they defiled the religion, mocked the movement, and fooled everyone. Some of them continue to do so today and get away with it.

John: Who do you mean?

Sufi: There are many, but the most flagrant example is that of the despicable House of Saud, truly the House of Idolaters, consisting of Fahd and his entourage of thieves, robbers, murderers, and usurpers of God's knowledge and providence, passing themselves off, with the help of friends like us—the United States of America, the European Union, and Japan—as deeply religious king and royal family and guardians of the holy mosques.

John: Who are the other ones?

Sufi: The list is long. Among some that come to mind and more or less equally culpable are Sabah of Kuwait, Husain of Iraq, Abdullah of Jordan, Asad of Syria, Mubarak of Egypt, Ghadafi of Libya, Taliban of Afghanistan and many small thugs who have nothing whatsoever to do with Islam, yet have done everything to advance their own interests in the name of Islam.

John: What about Iran?

Sufi: In the case of Iran, I have to admit that I was euphoric about the Islamic revolution brought about with the help of Imam Khomeni. But the euphoria was short-lived; it soon dissipated into disappointment and a great letdown. The signs of the demise of this revolution lay in the placards with pictures of Khomeni all over Iran. It didn't take long to realize this was no Islamic movement or revolution; it was simply a change of idol and continued idol worship.

Iranians may have been moved by the rhetoric of the Imam, but it was not the *movement* Islam that Khomeni was bringing; it was the *dead religion* Islam that was being imposed. An oppressive army of Mullahs and Imams who worshiped religion as god routed the movement that was to bring love, peace, and freedom for the citizens.

I kept hoping that Khomeni would denounce the placards of his image and the idol worship they symbolized, promoted, and reinforced, but he never did. It was naive of me to think that he would denounce even the system of clergy that is prohibited in Islam, but he never did. I thought he would announce the establishment of a true Islamic State—under One God of all the old religions but free of the religions themselves, with the purpose of life defined as the quest of God, not wealth—but he never did.

I thought he would announce the end to discrimination on the basis of gender and promote legislation for equality of laws with regard to marriage, divorce, and inheritance, but he never did.

And so we had in Iran a non-Islamic revolution that replaced the tyranny of monarchy with the tyranny of clergy, that continues after the death of Khomeni.

John: And Pakistan?

Sufi: Without speaking of the way that Pakistan, as a nation, reached its present state, I would say that the first step the Pakistanis can take to make theirs an Islamic State is to declare and practice a secular democracy. The second step is to accept the Mohajirs—the descendants of the misguided migrants of 1940s from India as their full citizens. Then accept the fact, declare to the world, and show that languages and regions are not the gods they worship. How can an Islamic State have so many "communities or divisions"?

John: Sufiji, aren't you being harsher on Islamic States than on others?

Sufi: You are right. They certainly do not have a monopoly on oppression and exploitation. In fact, the least suspected in our own eyes—ourselves—these United States of America are deeply involved in these practices implicitly or explicitly, overtly or covertly throughout the world in league with cohorts who have long pretended to be civilized. But at least a great

majority of them admit being what they are:
Materialists—Capitalists, Communists, or Socialists.
People who call themselves Muslims and nations
that call themselves Islamic have an added responsibility to live up to the expectation in fact and deed and
not to take the name of God in vain. I cannot think of
a greater crime against God than to call oneself
Muslim and not be one, or to claim to be an Islamic
State without being one. I sometimes wonder if the
Kaaba at Mecca has not become a monolithic idol and
the tombs of the dead intercessor idols for the misguided Muslims.

John: So the Hindus are not the only idol worshippers on the planet.
Sufi: Certainly not. We all are, regardless of our
professed or claimed religion. But unlike the idols
of Hinduism, that are intercessor gods, or simply
personifications of attributes of God, the idols of the
new religion Capitalism ended up being gods themselves.

John: Would you please comment further about
laws in the Koran that you think were meant for a specific time and space, as you put it, but were interpreted as if they were for all times and spaces.
Sufi: All laws in the Koran are derived from the
eternal principle, *"La ilaha illal Llah,"* that is, "There
is no god but God." The purpose of all laws is to cre-

ate a just and equitable society to enable Man to live a life of love, peace, and freedom.

The Koran, like other scriptures and books of God, is a book of guidance. Some laws in this sacred book were clearly intended and decreed to solve specific problems of the Sixth and the Seventh Century CE in the Arabia of Messenger Muhammad and took into consideration the local customs and traditions and most importantly showed a direction of change that was to continue until equity and justice were achieved. Some of these laws, for example, pertain to women and their just and equitable rights, obligations, and responsibilities.

At the time of Messenger Muhammad, women were treated as property and possessions of man. The laws of the Koran changed that radically. Men were restricted to marry no more than four women, contrary to the then current practice of marrying an unlimited number, under such a strict set of conditions that even its most liberal interpretation would prevent anyone from marrying more than one in our time and space. Nevertheless, far too many so-called Muslims have abused this conditional permission.

Now, equity and justice demand that these laws of polygamy be changed to those of monogamy and grant women the same rights with respect to divorce that men have.

Inheritance laws in the Koran gave women more than they had formerly been entitled to. The direction of the law was correct, and it should, by now, have reached full equity.

Unfortunately, what was meant as guidance to law making for specific purposes under specific circumstances was turned into unchangeable law for all times and spaces. The Islamic movement was thus thwarted and suffocated, becoming only a relic of the past because the Mullahs and the Ulamas, through their narrow minded, often self-serving (or ruler-serving) interpretations of the Koran and the sayings of Messenger Muhammad, froze the movement as it was at that time.

The interpretation of the Koran and of the sayings and the life of Messenger Muhammad is the responsibility of the individual Muslim; it cannot be relegated to the so-called learned, lest they become intercessors. It is for this reason that the clergy is outlawed in Islam. I cannot be held responsible for someone else's interpretation or action, nor can I justify my action based on someone else's interpretation. I may seek help from any and all in understanding and interpreting, but the ultimate responsibility is solely mine.

My statements about women in the so-called Islamic societies should not be considered an endorsement of their treatment and status in other societies; nowhere in the world have women achieved equality. And equality on the basis of gender is essential for achieving equality on every other basis.

John: Sufiji, what you are talking about applies equally to all other religions, too. Haven't the so-called "learned" in each religion become the interpreters and therefore intercessors in each religion?

Sufi: Yes. I was born in a Hindu family. In Hinduism, the Brahmin has always played the role of an intercessor. So you are correct in saying that the so-called learned in each religion have become intercessors. But do you know why these interpreters and intercessors are so popular and so much in demand?

John: Because we are preconditioned to the idea and the concept?

Sufi: Yes, and because the alternative is to accept, to take, the responsibility to learn, understand, and act on our own. We prefer to transfer or delegate this responsibility to someone else, donate some money instead (bribe?), plead ignorance, and restrict religious observance to rituals and dietary restrictions.

But the Koran tried to help Man put an end to these practices. As the story of the first revelation is related, Muhammad, in deep meditation, heard a voice say: "Read!" That was the first commandment or instruction of God to the newly appointed Messenger. Thus, *Koran*, an Arabic word meaning "Reading," became the title of the Sacred Book of Guidance. Throughout the book, Man is asked to read, observe, think, comprehend, understand, contemplate, meditate, and reflect on nature, history, and other books of

God sent through other Messengers of God. Man is to look for all the signs of God that abound in the Universe. Doing all that requires much work, apparently hard work. Instead of searching for the signs and the purpose and meaning of life, we search for ease, convenience, and comfort; we delegate the hard duties to the Priests, the Ministers, the Rabbis, the Mullahs, and the Pundits. Sadly, for a great majority of those poor souls, being one of the learned is just another job, an acceptable occupation or a profession.

John: What do we do then?

Sufi: We should ask ourselves several times everyday: Why am I here on this planet at this time? What is the purpose of my life?

John: Will it not be a frustrating experience because we may not get any satisfactory or acceptable answers at least in a short period of time?

Sufi: It will be a frustrating experience if we don't have patience. We are accustomed to instant answers, instant gratification. We would rather spend time in diversions and be absorbed in illusions than in meditation and contemplation.

John: Sufiji, is that why Muslims pray five or more times a day?

Sufi: That was the idea. I am glad you brought that up. The total time spent in the worship of God five times a day in the traditional manner would still be less than three hours a day. I understand that most people spend that much or more time watching television. It has often been charged or stated as a joke that people bow in worship before television sets.

But let's not assume that the so-called Muslims praying five times a day are finding God. For most of them, praying is merely a ritual and an obligation—more mechanical and physical than spiritual. You can prostrate yourself all you want, but if your mind is preoccupied with ways you are going to be wealthy or preserve the wealth you have accumulated or with any other desire, you are surely not worshipping the One God. And if such preoccupation continues between prayers, your worship is a self-deception.

The whole idea of worshipping five times a day, beginning before sunrise and ending after sunset with the day interrupted by three more sessions is to help Man keep focused on his purpose in life. It is very easy to become distracted by the material world that surrounds and overwhelms us. But worship has to be voluntary. The individual who has taken a vow of surrender and commitment, who has made a covenant of surrender to God, desires more than anything else to seek to experience the existence of God. What one does from habit or compulsion is not worship.

A long time ago, in India, I had a friend in high school who belonged to a small community of Muslims who believed that the controversially expected Messiah Mahdi had come and gone in Jaunpur, India, in the Fifteenth Century CE. I didn't find this friend or members of his community to be different from any other Muslims that I knew at the time except for one ritual that was unique to them. What my friend told me about Imam Mahdi and his teachings made an impression on me that is fresh even today. In fact, that narrative set me on the path of search through Islam, Hinduism—the religion of my parents—and all other religions.

The ritual is performed on the tenth day of the month of Moharram of the Muslim calendar. On that day, some fourteen hundred years ago, prophet Muhammad's grandson, Imam Husain, his family, and members of his party are believed to have asked God and each other for forgiveness before preparing for the battle, which turned out to be their last in which they were brutally massacred by the despotic ruler Yazid and his army of reprobates. Ever since, for the entire Muslim world, the day has become a day of mourning.

In remembering and observing this day, members of that tiny Mahdavi Muslim community, as they are called, go beyond mourning the cruel massacre. They awaken before sunrise to grant and ask each family member and God for forgiveness for any (wrongful) words spoken or deeds done to the other. They visit relatives and friends and exchange words of forgive-ness, saying: "For the sake of God, please forgive me for anything I may have said or done that hurt you or your feelings as I forgive you for any hurt that you may have caused me."

Forgiveness, however, was an everyday requirement and not just an annual ritual for Imam Mahdi. He preached that God would not accept our worship and prayers if the worshipper held any ill feelings or resentment against anyone; one had to cleanse heart and soul of malice through forgiveness before beginning worship or prayer. In addition to the five worship sessions a day, Imam Mahdi implored his followers to remember God in every breath, teaching them to say "there is no god," when exhaling and to say "but God," when inhaling. The Imam asked his followers not only to desire a vision (knowledge) of God but also to fill their hearts with that desire so that there is no room for any other desire. In addition to the creed, he further declared that his religion was based on the book of God and on following the Messenger of God.

The Mahdavi Muslims assumed that he meant the Koran and Muhammad to be the book and the Messenger in his declaration. But I think he meant all the Books of God and Scriptures including the Koran and all the Messengers of God including the last one, Muhammad.

John: Sufiji, why is Prophet Muhammad the last Messenger and greatest of them all?

Sufi: I think he is the last Messenger because there is no need for anymore. There is nothing more to add.

God has sent us the message in so many languages, to so many people through so many Messengers that no more Messengers are needed; it is all up to us now.

As for Muhammad the Messenger of God being the greatest of them all, that is simply a misconception. The Koran specifically says that God makes no distinction among prophets or Messengers of God; they are all of equal status.

John: Could we substitute the name of any prophet or Messenger for the name of Muhammad in the Creed, "There is no god but God; Muhammad is the Messenger of God"?

Sufi: Absolutely. In fact, Muhammad's name in the declaration implies the name of every Messenger of God. Muhammad's name is there to make certain that he (or any other Messenger of God) is not mistaken for or misunderstood later to be a god or anyone but a mortal Messenger.

John: What clarity and meaning you give, Sufiji. I always heard those words as a statement of Muhammad's exalted status, not as a classification of his role.

That brings to mind a concern I would like to share with you. Frankly and very bluntly, I must say that America and the West in particular, but in general the whole present day non-Muslim world, has a built-in bias against Muhammad the Messenger or

anything Islamic or Muslim. The very words *Islam*
and *Muslim* close their minds. That's why I was won-
dering whether one can somehow talk about "surrender" and not about Islam?

Sufi: I am glad you are sharing your concerns. It
is not the Arabic word *Islam* but the intent, the deed,
and the act of surrender that matter. So, yes, you can
substitute any word in any language that describes it.

Since we are talking about words and their meaning, your use of the expression "non-Muslim world"
presupposes a Muslim world. There are people who
call themselves Muslims, but there are no Muslims in
the strictest sense of the word. We are all idol worshippers; idol worship is a global phenomenon of our
time.

As for "America and the West," we have to get
such confines out of our minds. I know it is not easy,
but we need to start thinking of planet Earth without
boundaries and barriers of color, gender, race,
nationality, religion, language, and so on, because
all such means of selective inclusion and exclusion
become provincial gods that prevent us from seeking God.

Bias or prejudice against other people grows out
of ignorance—lack of knowledge. And the only way
to overcome ignorance is through knowledge—
knowledge of Love, Peace, and Freedom.

Muhammad is the friend of all Mankind—as is
every Messenger of God. Open up to him and to all

the Messengers of God and seek guidance and blessings from God.

Treat all religions as our religions because they are truly our inheritance—all of them. Look for similarities, commonalities, and the one unifying principle rather than distinctions, differences, and divisive schemes.

You will find what you are looking for, what you are after. If it is wealth you are after, you will find wealth; if it is God you are looking for, you will find God. Look for diversity, you will find diversity; look for unity, you will find unity.

John: Sufiji, as for borders and borderless world, what we see in the world at present is a trend toward, not away from, more borders. There are demands every day for separate states for different reasons—ethnic background, culture, language, tribe, religion. Over one hundred new countries came into being between World War II and the breakup of the Soviet Union, and twenty or so new countries have emerged since then. And how many more are waiting?

Then there are problems such as we have here in the United States with illegal immigrants coming from all over the world, especially from Latin America. If we move toward the desired world without borders, don't you think that would aggravate the problems of social turmoil and human misery?

Sufi: I agree with you. I am certainly not suggesting that we open the borders and create chaos, mayhem, and destruction.

We know that it is the idol Wealth that is attracting the rest of the world to the United States of America because, in a world of idol worshippers, America is the pilgrim center and the sacred abode of the gods themselves. But the United States is not alone to face this problem. Illegal migration has become a global phenomenon. The flow of migration is always from the underdeveloped to the developed countries, from the poor to the rich countries.

Politically, it is popular to raise our voice against the illegal immigrants. And no doubt, in societies based on laws, anyone who breaks the law must be punished in accordance with the laws, and the illegal immigrant must be deported to the country of his or her origin. We cannot afford to be a society in which lawbreakers are rewarded and law-abiding citizens as well as legal immigrants penalized.

But it seems to me that we are deliberately overlooking the "respectable" law breaking citizens who are employing, assisting in employment, or harboring the illegal immigrants. Do we really want to solve the problem of illegal immigration, or do we want to maintain a constant supply of cheap labor for dirty, difficult and unpleasant jobs?

We are eager to put the petty thief convicted of a felony three times behind bars for a minimum of twenty years and perhaps for life, but we let a major thief, in fact a robber, who continues to break the laws year in and year out by hiring illegal immigrants get away because he has the favor of the gods of capital, land, or manufacturing and can offer as ritual sacrifice contributions to the election campaign coffers of politicians.

Individuals or groups speaking for one side or the other raise questions about laws, ethics, and morality. As the global competition for raising or maintaining a higher standard of living increases, we keep adding laws because we need them to protect one god or other in an ever increasing population of gods; the need for this excessive number of laws is a sign of moral and ethical bankruptcy. But we fail to realize, to see, that idol worship by its very nature is unlawful, unjust, and without virtue, morality, or ethics.

John: Sufiji, that is a damning indictment of our legal system.

Sufi: The purpose of laws is to promote justice. The concept of justice begins with the legal assumption that all human beings are created equal, that all the resources of the planet are the property of God and our role is simply that of trustees, for which we receive enough—sufficient and adequate—resources for our survival. When everything in the universe and this planet belongs to God and is the property of God, my intelligence and your intelligence and the collective intelligences of Man are also the property of God.

If someone is not as intelligent as you are, you ought to be first and foremost thankful to God and second be compassionate and supportive of one who is not so endowed. But everyone has a gift from God in addition to the gift of life. It follows, therefore, that the resources of the Earth that are the blessings of God ought to be shared if not equally, at least equitably.

Just because I might be more intelligent than you are and able to think of clever ways in which I can gain advantage over you and many others like you, I should not have the right to do so. But that is exactly what we have done with our laws. We have made laws that reward my clever ways of thinking and taking advantage of you and others like you. How can anyone bring moral and ethical values to such an immoral and unethical system of laws that is devoid of any virtue to begin with?

John: What did you mean when you said "if not equally, at least equitably"?

Sufi: Equality—egalitarianism—is a sign of an Islamic State, a Rama Rajya, or the Kingdom of God on Earth, wherein every human being accepts responsibility equally, and everyone seeks only necessary and sufficient resources.

Until that happens, I think we would have to have some system of reward and incentive for acceptance of responsibility and various degrees of responsibilities. I am not sure what that system would be or should be. Perhaps some formula for the distribution of resources so that the richest could not receive more than ten or five times that which the poorest receive—and all would receive necessary and sufficient resources?

In that way or in some other way, I think we would need to begin by setting some kind of limit on the disparity of wealth between the rich and the poor, first within each country and then between countries, progressing by increments until the entire planet is an economically equitable society.

The idea of democracy of one person, one vote would be a sound system only in an economically equitable society; otherwise, the imbalance of power makes a mockery of democracy.

At this time in our world there is a tremendous inequity and imbalance both within countries and between countries. But nothing else can be expected in idol worship. We have to dismantle idol worship by surrendering to no god but God and by changing our laws to reflect our intent. That means doing away with the despicable Materialism: Capitalism and its Protestant movements, Communism and Socialism.

John: I wonder how far the idea of the same pay for any and all work can go when even equal pay for equal work hasn't gone very far.

Sufi: Change comes slowly. Slavery was endorsed by the government and blessed by the church for more than a century before there was a concerted movement to abolish it. Individuals and groups do complain about today's economic and political inequality, but they work to make the system operate in their favor—not to do away with the system. Disparity between pay for one's labor and recognition of one's real worth, will, in time, disappear—but not without great struggle.

John: Sufiji, I think you paint a very bleak picture. And the solution is scary.

Sufi: John, when the problem is idol worship, the only picture you can paint is bleak. You and I, sitting here, can say that the only solution is to surrender to One God, the Giver and Taker of life. What we can't say is that people would be willing to consider it, implement it, take the necessary steps. Those steps seem easy to me, but to idol worshippers who don't know or won't believe that they are worshipping idols, the steps may seem impossible or destructive of all they know.

Recall for a moment the Exodus and the disappointment of the Hebrews *after* leaving the deplorable life of slavery. What was heaven for Moses seemed wilderness to the Hebrews; what was a life of comfort in freedom and worship of One God to Moses seemed like hardship to the Hebrews because they still had not surrendered to the One God and had in fact reverted to worshipping a golden calf.

Or imagine the radical Jewish Revolutionary

Messiah and Messenger of God, Jesus. He wouldn't even stay at the Village Chief's house when invited but would stay at the house of the poorest of the poor. His admonition to his fellow Jews to abandon idol worship—worship of the oldest god, Wealth—and his invitation to the Jews and other inhabitants to join him in establishing the Kingdom of God on Earth would take him to the Cross without making a dent in the life of idol worship.

Today, the scenery has changed, but the problem and the solution have not. We need a daring, bold first step. Maybe we should ask the Imperial President of the United States to move out of the White House Palace and settle into the slums of D.C. and dismantle the palace, brick by brick, stone by stone. Build modest structures to conduct the law making business and the rendering of justice and dismantle in like fashion the Capitol and the Supreme Court buildings. Modesty must replace opulence.

Jesus, Moses, and Muhammad would refuse to enter any of these buildings; these monuments glorify Man, not God. They are the symbols of idol worship. We need to start there for the shock value.

John: Sufiji, people would simply laugh at the idea and think it a joke. At best, they would say it's impractical, don't you think?

Sufi: I am sure people would laugh at first. But look and read carefully the life stories of Jesus and

Muhammad, two of the Messengers of God we can find ample historical data on. Look especially at Muhammad because he did establish an Islamic State in his lifetime. He could have lived like a king of the kings, but he chose to live like the poorest of the poor.

I think the easiest route to the straight path is to follow in the footsteps of Jesus, Muhammad, and other Messengers of God. But as Lao-Tse said, "the Great Way is easy, yet people prefer by-paths." The straight path is always practical, but we call it impractical so we can devise sophisticated and complicated ways to pursue our base desires of idol worship.

~

Ahimsaji, who had looked sometimes at me, sometimes at the ocean as he talked, stopped talking and looked toward the horizon. The sound of the ocean became audible—as if it had been turned off while we talked. The moment seemed to call for silence, so I did not speak. After a few minutes, the Sufi asked how long it would take us to return to my place and how long it would take to go to the airport. He declined my invitation for dinner, saying that he would be served on the plane. He then pointed to a rock close to the shore and said that he would like to sit there and meditate until it was time to leave the beach, adding that we could talk more before his departure.

Our stop at my house was brief—as was the drive to the airport. There was enough time for me to express—or try to express—my pleasure and appreciation for his sharing his thoughts with me. He was so gracious he made it seem as if I had done something for him. The airport was close, and while he was checking in, I was checking my tape recorder. We were at his departure gate well before boarding time and found a place away from other passengers. The Sufi then resumed dialogue.

CHAPTER FOUR

Surrender as Solution

Sufi: What confusions have I created? What points need attention? Or is there a different place to start?

John: Sufiji, competing questions are crowding my brain. First, would I be correct in saying that our goal is to have a secular democratic government under One God but devoid of any religion?

Sufi: Well, democracy is no panacea, and government is never a goal for those who surrender to God; a democratic government to them is always and only a means to preserve order as we are establishing the Kingdom of God on Earth. After that, we pursue our goal—the purpose of life—to seek God.

To speak of government being devoid of any religion, we must avoid being caught in a semantic trap. Government must certainly be devoid of both the old and the new religions, and it certainly would be if its function remained as we just defined it, but, as we have already said, when people look to a government to make decisions about ways of life or to solve problems, government itself becomes a religion. The difficulty does not end there, for the practitioners of the old religions use all political means available to gain advantage and privilege from the new religion—the government. The new religion does not recognize itself as a religion but thinks it is the instrument that protects all religions without any preferences. As Gandhi said, people who believe religion has nothing to do with politics, that is, government, do not know what religion is.

Jesus told us without any ambiguity, "No one can serve two masters; for either he will hate the one and love the other, or he will hold to one and despise the other. You cannot serve God and Mammon."

The idea of separation, that we can have one set of laws and rules for the old religion and another one for the new religion and follow both is a ridiculous one; it is tantamount to legalizing hypocrisy and deception. Furthermore, by giving the power of enforcement to the laws of the new religion—the government—the old religions have become decorative lion guardians on each side of the gate to the house of worship for the gods of the new religion.

John: What do you think we can or should do now?

Sufi: If we wish to make changes, to reverse the polytheistic laws, we certainly have all the tools and the institutions available to us. But the first step in taking such a course is to accept the responsibility and not try to shift it to an earlier generation. A historical background is useful in determining the way we arrived at the place we now stand upon, but only the acceptance of responsibility can empower us to make the necessary changes.

And this time around it is not enough to make changes within confined boundaries of nation states; it is imperative that we work both within and without to remove all artificial boundaries and barriers such as nations, religions, languages, color, gender.

John: Could the United States of America serve as a model to be extended to the entire world: the United States of Planet Earth?

Sufi: Yes, but a model of a reformed United States of America—a state minus Materialism/ Capitalism, with necessary and sufficient governments at both the state and federal levels, a new declaration of freedom for Man, a declaration of interdependence for neighbors, and a mission statement of the purpose and the meaning of life.

John: What do you mean by necessary and sufficient government?

Sufi: The best government is that which allows and helps its citizens to govern themselves. We need as much government as is necessary and only as much as is sufficient to accomplish our purpose. We all realize and recognize that our own governments have become too big and are still getting bigger. People are calling for smaller governments. But the work on reducing the power of the government must accompany the work on reducing the power of the corporation, the power of the individual, and the power of the groups of individuals. Reducing one without reducing the other is as dangerous as leaving them as they are. Each by itself or all together, they rob us of our freedoms throughout the world.

John: What about the argument that more government is necessary to provide services for its citizens, especially for the poor and the underprivileged?

Sufi: Government must not be allowed to provide any services on a permanent basis or even over a long period of time other than maintaining an infrastructure for the common good of all. Any other services that a government provides for whatever reason must be for a short period such as during an emergency when no other alternatives are available.

Social Security benefits that were instituted during the depression, for example, may have been desirable at the time as emergency measures, but they should not have been institutionalized nor made into a permanent system. And, recognizing the fallacy of the system, I must be provocative enough to say that we should take immediate steps to bring the system to an end by returning to all the participants their total contributions—with a fair return if possible.

The evils of the welfare system are becoming apparent to everyone. The system promotes irresponsibility of the individual and makes government bigger and more powerful. It must be abolished, but so must the tax breaks for the rich and the powerful, which, shrouded in respectable words, are a form of welfare for the wealthy.

As for the redistribution of wealth, it is a myth. There is no historical evidence it has ever been accomplished and is impossible to achieve in a society of idol worshippers. Our goal should not be redistribution of wealth anyway; it should be prevention of accumulation of wealth—making redistribution unnecessary.

John: What about charity? Isn't a welfare system for the poor a form of forced charity by way of taxation?

Sufi: Charity is voluntary; tax is mandatory. I

think the essential elements of the welfare system for the poor, that is, helping neighbors in need, should be taken over by neighborhood charities, which should help those in need help themselves to become responsible free citizens. I think a good rule to observe in charity is: Everyone must give, but no one should ask.

John: Sufiji, you are very different from any other Sufi that I have read or heard about. Most Sufis have confined themselves to the spiritual and said little about the material world, much less the political world of Man.

Sufi: You might say I am redefining Sufism. A Sufi is a lover of God. How can a Sufi see this worldwide worship of every little god but God and not wage a Crusade, a Jihad, or a Satyagraha against idol worship?

John: With the name "Ahimsa," you are surely not suggesting any renewal of violence, but the words *Crusade* and *Jihad* conjure up images of violent confrontations and wars, particularly between Christians and Muslims from the centuries gone by.

Sufi: The days of violence should have ended a long time ago. Unfortunately, wars and violent confrontations are still with us, and we need to promote non-violence as a way of life.

I know it has been widely misinterpreted, but Crusade, Jihad, or Satyagraha is a nonviolent struggle for Truth, that is, Love, Peace, and Freedom. It is a struggle for the worship of no god but God, a struggle against our base desires of idol worship. It is a struggle for justice, equity, and equality.

John: Then what do you think about the slogans of Jihad raised in many parts of the world?

Sufi: I think they are all campaigns for one god or other, gods such as nation, language, religion, or land; I don't know of any struggle that qualifies as Jihad.

John: You are not condemning all the struggles, are you?

Sufi: I am suggesting that all the current struggles in the world are incomplete and misguided at best. The only true struggle that can liberate Man from every conceivable bondage, tyranny, oppression, and pollution is to surrender to no god but God, the Lord of the Worlds, and move to establish the Kingdom of God on Earth.

John: Sufiji, I appreciate your time and patience with me. More questions are coming to my mind, and I hope I will have another opportunity to spend some time with you.

Sufi: God willing. In the meantime, determine whether *you* can answer all the questions yourself in the light of the principle, "There is no god, but God." Therein lie all the answers and the solutions to all the problems.

When the first boarding announcement was made, the Sufi said his farewell as he hugged me on each shoulder. I felt my eyes getting wet.

"Goodbye, Sufiji," I said as I held his right hand with both of mine.

"Goodbye, John," the Sufi said, "may God bless us all with love, peace, and freedom, and let's work to establish the Kingdom of God on Earth."

I watched the Sufi board the plane. I stood at the window until the plane taxied out to the runway, paused, rolled forward, and rose into the air.

Sermon On The Mount

Blessed are the poor in spirit,
   for theirs is the kingdom of heaven.
Blessed are those who mourn,
   for they shall be comforted.
Blessed are the meek,
   for they shall inherit the earth.
Blessed are those who hunger and thirst for
   righteousness, for they shall be satisfied.
Blessed are the merciful,
   for they shall receive mercy.
Blessed are the pure in heart,
   for they shall see God.
Blessed are the peacemakers,
   for they shall be called sons of God.

Selection from *Sermon on the Mount*; Matthew 5:3-9
New American Standard Bible, 1972, The Lockman Foundation

The Eightfold Path

as revealed through Gautama Buddha,
The Messenger of God

1. Right Understanding, View or Knowledge
2. Right Thoughts, Motives, Intentions or Attitude
3. Right Speech
4. Right Action or Behavior
5. Right Means of Livelihood or Vocation
6. Right Effort
7. Right Concentration or Mindfulness
8. Right Meditation or Concentration

NOTE: The word 'Right' is also described as 'Perfect,' implying highest quality.

ADAPTED FROM:
(1) *Buddhist Scriptures.* Trans. Edward Conze. London: Penguin Books, 1959. p 110;
(2) Humphreys, Christmas. *Buddhism.* 3rd. ed. London: Penguin Books, 1962. p 114;
(3) *The Teachings of Buddha.* Tokyo: Bukkyo Dendo Kyokai, 1966, p 37.

The Ten Commandments

as revealed to Moses, The Messenger of God

1. You shall have no other gods before Me.
2. You shall not make for yourself a graven image; [You shall not surrender to them or worship them.]
3. You shall not take the name of God, your Lord, in vain.
4. Remember [Me on] the Sabbath day, to keep it holy [by concentrating and meditating on Me.]
5. Honor your father and your mother.
6. You shall not kill or murder.
7. You shall not commit adultery.
8. You shall not steal.
9. You shall not bear false witness against your neighbor.
10. You shall not covet [desire, especially material possessions].

NOTE: The brackets, and the words therein, have been added to enhance new interpretations

ADAPTED FROM:
(1) *New American Standard Bible.* La Habra, California: The Lockman Foundation, 1960 p 99, 241;
(2) *The World Almanac and Book of Facts* 1994. Mahwah, NJ. p 731.

APPENDIX 3

Surrender
as revealed through Krishna,
The Messenger of God

■ The giving up of work prompted by desire is called renunciation; the abandonment of the reward or the fruit of all work is called surrender.

■ Some say that action should be given up, since action disturbs contemplation, but others say that acts of sacrifice, gift, and penance or self-harmony should not be given up.

■ Hear now the truth about surrender: Surrender is of three kinds.

■ Works of sacrifice, gift, and penance or self-harmony should not be abandoned but should indeed be performed; for these are works of purification.

■ But even these works, should be performed, giving up attachment and desire for fruits or rewards. This is my final word.

ADAPTED FROM:

(1) *The Bhagavad-Gita*. Trans. S. Radhakrishnan. New York: Harper Torchbooks, 1973. pp 351-353;
(2) *The Bhagavad-Gita*. Trans. Juan Mascaro. Middlesex: Penguin Books, 1962. pp 115-116.

Glossary

Many words of languages other than English, have been defined and explained in the book, but some are included here again for easy reference. When the origin of the foreign language word is known, it is indicated in parenthesis. In some instances new meanings or explanations have been given to words and have been placed in brackets for such identification.

Abd *(Arabic)* Literally, worshiper; slave, servant.

Abdallah *(Arabic)* Worshiper, slave or servant of God.

Abraham *(Late Latin)* From Greek *Abraam*, from Hebrew *Abhraham; Ibrahim* in Arabic; 2nd millennium BCE patriarch; progenitor of the Jews through son Isaac and of the Arabs through another son Ishmael; the Koran names Abraham as the Messenger of God who rebuilt Kaaba in Mecca and established pilgrimage to Mecca.

Ahimsa *(Sanskrit)* Devoid of violence; nonviolence.

Allah *(Arabic)* God; Bhagawan; Ishvar; YHWH (Yahweh); Elohim.

Asoka Asoka the Great, the king of Magadha (273-232 BCE) who adopted Buddhism as State religion and became a missionary.

Aum *(Sanskrit)* Also Om; the sacred syllable representing the impersonal Absolute as well as the personal aspect of God.

BCE Before Common Era.

Bhagavadgita *(Sanskrit)* Literally, "Song of the Blessed" is the Gospel of Hinduism. Dated between the 5th and 2nd Centuries BCE, the Gita comprising 18 chapters, is a part of Mahabharata. In the form of a dialogue between [Messenger of God] Krishna and his friend and disciple Arjuna, it teaches how to achieve union with the Supreme Reality (God) through the paths of knowledge, devotion, meditation and surrender.

Bible The sacred scriptures comprising the Old Testament, sacred to both the Jewish and Christian faiths and the New Testament, acknowledged only by Christians; both the Old and the New Testaments are referred to as the "Books of God" in the Koran.

Brahmin *(Sanskrit)* A member of the priestly Hindu class (caste) responsible for officiating at religious rites and studying and teaching the scriptures.

Brahma *(Sanskrit)* God of Creation; [Creator, an attribute of God, Ishvara; one of the trinity of attributes of God].

Buddha *(Sanskrit)* 'The enlightened one;' Siddhartha

Gautama 563B CE to 483 BCE; Founder of Buddhism; Reformer of Hinduism; [Messenger of God; through whom were revealed the Four Noble Truths and the Noble Eightfold Path; Gautama Buddha did not talk of 'God' because God is beyond any words or description; One can only strive to experience the existence of God].

Caliph From *Khalifah (Arabic)*; Successor, Substitute, Deputy.

CE Common Era.

Copernicus Nicholaus Copernicus (1473-1543), Polish astronomer, best known for his astronomical theory that the earth, spinning on its axis once daily, revolves annually around the sun, challenging the then universally held belief that the earth was stationary and motionless at the center of several concentric rotating spheres that included the sun, the moon, and other planets of our solar system.

Das *(Sanskrit)* Servant, slave.

Dhammapada *(Sanskrit)* Literally *pada* means 'the way' and *dhamma* means 'the teaching;' hence, "The Path of Truth;" attributed to Gautama Buddha; scripture of Buddhism.

Gandhi Mohandas Karamchand Gandhi (1869-1948 CE), popularly known as the 'Mahatma' (the

Great Soul); a true follower of the world's great religions, Gandhi walked into the footsteps of all the Messengers of God from Manu [Adam] to Muhammad.

Gautama *(See Buddha)*

God A distinction is made between God (with capital letter G) to denote the One God—the God of all religions and god or gods (with small case letter g) to denote the false, many, or lesser powers created by God or Man; *(See Allah and Ishvara)*.

Guru *(Sanskrit)* Teacher; expert; a religious leader.

Hindu *(Persian/Sanskrit)* Derived from the Sanskrit word *Sindhu,* "river", more specifically, the Indus; the Persians in the 5th century BC called the inhabitants of the land of Indus, Hindu; currently used to identify an adherent of Hinduism.

Hinduism *(Persian/Sanskrit)* [One of the oldest monotheistic religions]; an amalgam of traditions and rituals, of devotional and philosophical systems built up over 4,500 years arising from indigenous (Dravidians or Indus Valley) cults and successive invasions, notable among which was that by the Aryans (c 2000-1500 BCE)

Husain *(Arabic)* Also Husayn; 624-680 CE; the grandson of prophet Muhammad; Imam Husain.

Imam *(Arabic)* A religious leader.

Ishvara *(Sanskrit)* Also Ishvar, Ishwar, Ishwara; God; Allah; Elohim; YHWH (Yahweh)

Ishvaradas *(Sanskrit)* Servant of God; Abdallah.

Islam *(Arabic)* Literally, "surrender", "reconciliation" from the word *salaam*, "peace" or "salvation".

Jesus *(Late Latin)* From Greek *Iesous*, from Hebrew *Yeshua*; the Jewish religious teacher whose life, death, and resurrection as reported by the Evangelists are the basis of the Christian message of salvation; also called *Jesus Christ*; the Koran says that Jesus (*Isa* in Arabic) was born of Virgin Mary, that he is a 'Spirit from God,' and the 'Word of God'; His titles, in the Koran, include *Messiah, prophet, Messenger of God,* and *'one of those brought nigh* (to God)'

Ji *(Hindi)* A word of respect that may be added to any person's name; Similar in meaning to 'Esquire'.

Kaaba *(Arabic)* Also Kabah; literally "cube"; the large cubic stone structure containing the Black Stone in one corner stands in the center of the Grand Mosque of Mecca; Neither the stone nor the Kabah are objects of worship but they represent a sanctuary consecrated to God since time immemorial and it is toward the kaaba that Muslims throughout the world orient themselves in worship and prayer; considered a spiritual center, a support for the concentration of consciousness upon the Divine Presence.

Kabir A mystic poet and reformer (1440-1518 CE) of both Hinduism and Islam, he scorned the rituals of both religions, the idolatry of the Hindus and the theological infighting of the Muslims. Refined the concepts of *Ahimsa* in Jainism and Buddhism and emphasized truth, compassion, and self-control; popular with the masses and persecuted by the ruling class, he is believed to have had a profound influence on Guru Nanak.

Koran *(Arabic)* al-*qur'aan*, literally "reading," or "recitation;" the sacred book (of guidance) of Islam.

Krishna *(Sanskrit)* [The Messenger of God and] teacher of Arjuna, in the epic poem 'Bhagavad-Gita'.

Lao-Tze *(Chinese)* Also: Lao-tse, Lao-tzu or Lao-zi; 6th Century BCE Chinese philosopher [mystic and a Messenger of God] regarded as the founder of Taoism (the way).

Mahdi *(Arabic)* Literally, "one who is rightly guided." Although not accepted by all, some Muslims believe that a Messiah Mahdi will come before Jesus and before the end of the world to help establish the Kingdom of God; Many have claimed to be *the* Mahdi, notable among them are Syed Muhammad of Jaunpur, India (1443-1505 CE); Muhammad Ahmad of Sudan (1843-1885 CE); Mirza Ghulam Ahmad of Qadian, India (1835-1908 CE).

Man With capital letter M, used in place of human being (gender neutral).

Mecca *(Arabic)* The city, in present day Saudi Arabia, in which the Kaaba and the Grand Mosque are located.

Moses *(Latin)* From Hebrew *Mosheh*, Arabic Moosa; 14th or 13th Century BCE Prophet and Messenger of God accepted as such by Jews, Christians and Muslims.

Muhammad *(Arabic)* Literally, "the praised one." The last Prophet and Messenger of God according to the Koran and Islamic beliefs; 570-632 CE.

Mullah(s) *(Arabic)* A religious leader; an expert.

Muslim *(Arabic)* Literally, "One who has surrendered (to God)", from *aslama*, "to surrender, to seek peace".

Namaz *(Persian)* Same as Salah.

Nanak Generally considered to be the founder of Sikh religion, Nanak Chand (1469-1538 CE) was the first of the ten Gurus; Guru Nanak started his mission with a simple statement: 'There is no Hindu, there is no Mussulmaan, only servants of God.'

Narada *(Sanskrit)* Hindu saint, mentioned in the Veda and other scriptures [Messenger of God].

Rajya *(Sanskrit)* Kingdom.

Rama *(Sanskrit)* 1. A name of God; [Derived from two attributes of God: Compassionate *(Rahman in Arabic)* and Merciful *(Rahim in Arabic)*]; Variation: Ram. 2. [Name of the Messenger of God; aka Ramachandra]

Rama Rajya *(Sanskrit)* Kingdom of God.

Rishi *(Sanskrit)* Enlightened seer saint; any of the ancient Hindu seers of spiritual truth, to whom knowledge of the Vedas was revealed; [Messenger of God].

Salah *(Arabic) Canonical* or ritual prayer; worship; spiritual and ritual surrender; Variation: Salat; similar to Yoga.

Satya *(Sanskrit)* Truth.

Sikh *(Sanskrit)* Shishya (disciple) became Sikh in Punjabi language; A follower of an uncompromising monotheistic religion founded by Guru Nanak and shaped by nine Gurus that followed; Scripture: 'Granth Sahib,' compiled by the fifth Guru, Arjun, consists of over 6000 verses including writings of Guru Nanak and Kabir.

Siva *(Sanskrit)* Also Shiva; god of destruction, dissolution, transformation; [Destroyer (of worldliness), an attribute of God, Ishvara; One of the trinity of the attributes of God].

Sufi *(Arabic)* A Muslim mystic; man of wool—from their woolen garment.

Surah *(Arabic)* A chapter of the Koran.

Ulama *(Arabic)* Plural of Aalim—the educated and the knowledgeable (in religion)

Upanishad *(Sanskrit)* Any of a group of philosophical treatises explicating Vedic knowledge; sacred Hindu scriptures.

Valmiki *(Sanskrit)* Hindu sage [Messenger of God]; considered the author of the ancient epic and the sacred text, Ramayana, the story of Rama [the Messenger of God]

Vardhamana *(Sanskrit)* the given name of "Mahavira", the title, literally, "the great hero," given to the last of the twenty four "Jinas" or "victorious ones"—great teachers who showed the path of salvation—commonly known as "Jainism;" the followers are called "Jains;" [Messenger of God]

Veda *(Sanskrit)* Vedah, literally "sacred lore," "wisdom," "knowledge;" any of the oldest Hindu sacred texts composed in Sanskrit and gathered into four collections.

Vidyarthi *(Sanskrit)* Seeker of knowledge; student.

Vishnu *(Sanskrit)* Literally, "the all-pervading;" Preserver; The Sustainer God; [Sustainer, an attribute of God, Ishvara; One of the trinity of attributes of God].

Vyasa *(Sanskrit)* Literally, arranger of the Vedas. Sage of great antiquity [Messenger of God]; considered the author of the *Mahabharata*, an ancient epic including the *Bhagavad Gita*, literally, *Song of the Blessed One*, the Sacred Hindu Scripture.

Yoga *(Sanskrit)* A spiritual union; a system of meditation involving physical and mental disciplines; Similar to Salah.

Zoroaster *(Persian)* also Zarathustra, the 6th Century BCE Persian prophet [and Messenger of God]; founder of Zoroastrianism.

Zoroastrianism *(Persian)* [One of the oldest monotheistic religions] founded by Zoroaster; followers of Zoroaster are called Zoroastrians.

O R D E R   F O R M

Star Publications

Please send _____ copy/copies of *A Sufi's Ruminations On*
One World Under God

PRICE: U.S. $10.00 / CANADA $13.00

Shipping & handling (S&H) is $4.00 for the first book, $2.00 each additional. California residents add 8.25% sales tax. International: $9.00 for the first book, $5.00 for each additional.

PRICE	_____
S & H	_____
SALES TAX	_____
TOTAL	_____

NAME

ADDRESS

CITY   STATE   ZIP

TELEPHONE   FAX

EMAIL

PAYMENT:

❑ Make checks payable to: Star Publications
   Mail to: P.O. Box 6175, San Pedro, CA 9734-6175, USA

❑ VISA ❑ MasterCard

Cardnumber:_____
Name on card:_____
Exp. Date: (mo) _____ (year)_____

■ Toll free order phone 1-866-THE SUFI (866-843-7834)
   Give mailing/shipping address, telephone number, MC/Visa name,
   address where statement is received and card number plus
   expiration date.
■ Fax orders: 310-514-2148. Fill out this form & fax.
■ Order Online: orders@star-publications.com